posthumous remorse

&

a volume of painted prosody

shepperd rourke

© 2022

part one

"i was not; i was; i am not; i do not care." epicurus

"thoughts in time and out of season. the hitchhiker stood by
the side of the road.

   and levelled his thumb.

      in the calm calculus of reason."
jim morrison

     "tryna keep you out the crossfire"

      props to a humbling re-
minder.

part one prologue

i put a joker card with a black horse on it inside a copy of the sun also rises and set the book down on the nightstand & took out from the night-stand drawer a charcoal-colored leather pouch containing pre-cut aluminum foil, two-hollowed out pens, some lighters, a grip, and about a brick of heroin.

i folded the doubled-down aluminum foil into a thimble-sized cup. i then rested the tip of the flame under the cup for to cook and watched it stir and rise aways. i drew up the smoke thru the hollowed-out pen slow and deep, felt it thorough and encapsulate. i looked up & saw feeling. i then laid back. embraceable you.

1.

paneling soul

       whether zipper blues or dope dick

                        restless

                            spoonless & zenlike ad-
visements

tyranny of time & a ceramic bind on a concrete slab of virtuoso and perdition violinic stare and cold coffee pursuing

having tried might and the silvered plight of

                        hallowed angels

                          a   layover

awaiting tonic poured
                as
pontious pious spiked the main deep watching
  blood corroborate titillating euphoric
         a hungry fuck of a retards spiraling descent over
           a marooning catalyst
     and
          misanthropic rage being let like blood out over
             canvassed sheets spread to dra-
pery
            the flooring

   and
                    while
repainting remorse
    of did a number on them
      and did a fuckin number on them this time
        and recycling words by definition
as emotions still

      haven't and may never
corralled faithless they rocked off they sexuals
   and justine and magdelena cried fisted cards
    played on morphines upper plausible etcetera

morning hit with crystalline dick and piss spilt
   of high whore
     after hours and noon recalled recoiling upward vehe-

ment slap of brick wall ornate beautiful

                     sickly beautiful

            the solidified & solicitous rat that scrawled

for

                  some seconds on pious' head as he

lay dreaming

      with a scurrying rhythmic calm about smiles he had

sought

    and the crying burden of death that

bemused all nightly thought

you should see

    long loosed strideful

      too long in a day soon

a gospel in accordance with smack

     lugubriously dropped hatter

        archetypal delirium as inherit the belief that

           a moses parted sea

nat turner was misled by brailled pamphlet

      scrawled jesus

          while

            dionysian festivals adorned the pretty

                and

            "fuck you call me?"

              slap!

             "fuck you say?"

slap!

inherent the often

tongue starfish scrolled the gospel

drink balls disarrayed the pamphlet in

exclamation

as

the pretty ones of too long boldly

excavate

(an)

in our time

we stole time like bastards of the holy

muscle

black roses & hues

she knelt in ambrosias den for pious to stand

before

you silken black & you on your

knees

didn't mean you who

dream to please

(an)

predestined déjà vu

hatter set

i do

composition sitting pretty

strangered brew welled up in the eyes

and listened till they died

           a different justine and magdelena
                crying cards of segue &

protection

         the brick wall didn't deny anything

2.

correcting them when they were wrong about
    incidentals
        admitted to what they didn't have in substance
     as
        it's simply the outside looking in
       on
          (an)
            in our time

&

    we did our living outside the foundational box

       came "home" to crash as kids

         there's an incorrigible longing in our av-
enues

          & travels

as

    there is indirectly only one way in all we live

           in yearn

      and there is yield in those with hope

        (as) we, lifelong & aging addicts with our
ghosts so

          tangible that their privacy re-
mains constantly

            raped

         we yield if we hope

     &

      palpably yearning for ghosts and yielding for-
ward

        and how absolutely fucking beautiful
sickly

         beautiful addiction is

        there isn't much of anything
without it and there

    never was or could be

             world
without end

    and a glass cock

setting relativistic next to forged scripts for
    pain meds
        & saved from a hot dose of junk by a pin
        of crystal meth
          as
                fronted via forged checks
    &
        peace compromises
          and spotted local surveillance decades ago and
            spoke in roundabouts of indirect evasion
with
            charm

                didn't say shit
              haven't said much of a word in
              over twenty years now

              a posthumous remorse

&

    pushed away and lost the first two of five fiancées

       and forged scripts of pain meds

         to boot the cover

           dropped acid and wrote books

            lost grip temporarily

              and was briefly institutionalized &
stabilized

                resumed the junk, drinks,
writing

    and raids from local law enforcements

in decades of binge use of illicit drugs and the constancies of
alcohol

        as

           fuck off into a sock

              go out and bag a groupie or
fuck a hooker

                & come back to a
failed relationship

the law never found the firearms they were looking for

     & the mother of my child summed it up best

        it's all drugs and crime

as a baudelairean rose hides its scent

in the flowers of lubricity

primal instincts

societally denied

&

nothing but charm from this motherfucker

&

if you'd the eyes of the hawk and the senses of the wolf

you'd see that

I'm fucking good, sir

3.

you, who put a child before a statue of a half-naked fanatically criminal jew dead on a cross

you diabolique how are you sane? how can anyone fail to see that you are cruel and abusive?

you, who then tell the child to symbolically drink his blood and eat his body? to save the child's soul?

you, how are you not perpetuating a dangerous inanity and a violent insanity?

its child abuse.

its fundamental evil on many levels   where is the humanity and the logic?

jesus existed, was a fanatic philosopher, and was executed via capital punishment because he wouldn't shut the fuck up after having pissed off the wrong powerful people. i, personally, am genuinely heartbroken, and get an appalled nausea as to theists lack of sound logic and evidence, their convenient blindness and psychotic justifications as to the pervasively cruel, prejudiced, immoral, and largely violent fiction in and of, bible.

it is a proof that the fundamentally psychotic mediocrity govern the world. and while cannibalistic and circular in its dysfunction, it is, as yet, structurally essential. as yet, archetypal, for the fearful and the impotent, the internal failures in need of the metaphysical.

a celebrated inanity where cultures in an attempt to laugh so as not to be laughed at   and cultures that would construct a genocide if only the latest thing to do was to construct one   and GOD and NAZI megaphones mesmerizing meat cultures into an autonomous and global self-inflicted beheading.

in the impossible, we trust   politics feed on the mediocre   and the mediocre need structuring politics   it's a necessary and circular dysfunction.

they very often have very little insight and understanding of who it is their voting for and why   and   not very many are satisfied with the systems, as they are, decade after decade, in an unchanging complaint(s)

they just plaintive murmur like a queef out they opinions based on dick.

as mediocrity in every sect regurgitate the phrasings

as to their oppositions puppetry

in cannibalistic rhetoric

saying little to nothing, at best

and handshake

and cocksuck

they are the multitudinous fuckshit   the circle jerk of primeval continuity of pending war   the meat wagon mausoleum for the heart in logic

how, logically, is it not a contributing factor for instability in a primal culture when the rudiments of upbringing include disgusting, baseless justifications for symbolic cannibalism and judgements?

would lawlessness be a more utopian or dystopian society in a country of religious people? would lawlessness be a more utopian or dystopian society in a country of atheists?

not at all for nothing at all   and granted that within the reported percentages, there are variations and factors involved to a point, in 8 of the 10 safest countries in the world, the majority of the population is non-religious/atheist around 2020 i.e. (czech republic, japan, switzerland, austria, canada, denmark, new zealand, iceland.)

not at all for nothing at all   the top 10 most dangerous countries are very largely religious 80-100% with contributing factors believe in god. i.e. (india, syria, libya, nigeria, democratic republic of congo, iraq, pakistan, somalia, yemen, and afghanistan.)

i had never thought of the horrors of religion

while on junk and eating

pussy.

i'm sayin.

4.

aphoristic cantos

4.1

if i were possessed of

omnipotence and omniscience

and i were to create

a world with

struggle and evil

in it

i would be deemed

a

sadist.

4.2

poetics on the problem of evil

an incubus

having hit up virgin mary

explaining itself

in

scriptural denial.

4.3

this god will exist or not exist

regardless of our earthly ramblings

or intellectual digestions.

4.4

question the heart and the motive behind a

person who believes
in hell; eternal damnation.

4.5

the cause or occasion of dying

inexorable chasm

the denotation of death.

4.6

can god create a stone he can't lift?

circular paradoxes obfuscate some,

from etymological certainty, while

fruitless in their having

accomplished nothing more than

clever & onanistic wordplay

as

granted
there can never be any
evidence of a manifest
omnipotence.

omnipotence is as god
&
scientifically unprovable

conceptual fictions

4.7
the sorrows of a sodomite
as remorseless as the tides of the ocean
mourning piss spilt of high whore.

4.8
the non-linear cantos in the life of sensational
admixture where touching is heard

4.9
spent

religions vagina is roast beef

words deconstructed

misconstrued and translated into notes of deicide

4.10

the whiskey distillation fires a bleach without reti-
cence

as in anyone who looks into my eyes is a victim

the sleeping intensity in an alchemy of somno-
lence

4.11

the

sifted & silent

soft of a dropper manifested

4.12

else notes of genocidal aphorism

sisyphean logic need got soma

4.13

he thinks he is a glass of orange juice

he will not let you touch him as you might spill him

4.14

soma for sisyphus

&

a hope that there's good in the heart of what gets you thru the night

4.15

with no evidence of its existence

how can a good and sane person

believe in the endless cruelties of hell?

4.16

the concept of hell

an undying paradigm

as to

man's inhumanity to man

4.17

a thought-penny

i was never concerned

with christians

&

other horrors

while eating pussy

in the

sidereal tides

of russian roulette

and

a

pin of fent

4.18   sisyphean
positivity & affirmation   a decapitated individual processing
orgasmic thoughts

before losing consciousness

4.19 solipsistic mir-
rors in the caskets of the self-centered dead

4.20

logical hedonism

a cozy eudaimonic soma

for those would rather burn in hell

than live the plaintive baselessness of a life believ-
ing in it & eating jesus

i ain't sucking balls

4.21

pages of poetic brush-strokes & vignettes
of a posthumous remorse

5.

i need no excuse to go to atlantic city for a hooker
        while epicurean moderation advises
                principled blueprints accompanied
                        a base line & paroxysmal pissings
better hit her
        graphic packaging
                when you could understand   this sip and
                        that strike   of coruscating footnote
                                a blanket on the page
her cake is eaten too
        accustom thyself
                titillating tongue given to starfish
impious massage flickering an absence of thought
        ripe for rum poured thin   meanderings
                oscillating   & water-coloured imagery
                        methodical   post-traumas
aphoristic

poetries in charcoal outlined
        of synonymous intoxication(s)
            firing at the acoustics of metabolism
the patterns of seasick virgins in a charnel heart choir
        & bemusement(s) of dreamt away
            avenues of propitiatory acquiescence
                & then they leave out the spot
as some silhouettes of all sorts of past tense
                "fuck you say?"
                slap

              "fuck you say to me?"
                slap

tell you what to do
        bemusements
            bad cake, that
              free will is an illusion
                primal energies scar
tissue kittens & pawned engagements
the horns of sacrifice & forgot a line of concupiscence
    so spat like a blind pig & use your sense
        while into a drop of tap water
          & naturally fed to liquify the potent(s)   in
the spoon

while coruscant

two perfectly shaped ice cubes
       & us in time & fleshy spirit in
          distilled apparition
impartially boxed up with
     one foot forward   in the middle of the road
        before the morning comes   the sifted
& silent distillation of dropper manifest
     a blood let & the replacement
        as ode to sacrifice

invoke the feel
   & a bridge between as

          beyond good and evil
          the internal fireworks
          natures literature
         in a harmonious retribution
             &
   a noted nod from a dope hat as the world can't got
green

just another set of diamonds couldn't unify as one
     in a half dozen or so
        and one continued on & shone   descend-
ing
         in the paved harmonics of a
soloists
     livewire meeting & denotation of death

                                                        as   a
chasm inexorable

                            religions vagina is roast beef
                                words deconstructed
                            translated into notes of deicide

sound a track
      for a melancholy baby
            invoke the feel
                                    of an inspiration

two perfectly shaped ice cubes
      you put two perfectly shaped ice cubes
            in the glass
                  on the wooded table

over there
                              the dim light shines there on the wood
                        with coruscations of clarity
thesis titled
            the damage done
                  serenity   purchased
effigy
                                    resolute in a seat of thought
ladies and gentleman
            mr thelonious monk

atypical rhythmic calm & responding

obfuscate the sentience   in

riddling a 13th step

and

sheltered from moonlight   by

internal scars

 you want?

need as ubiquitous   looks

doubly confined   in the naked stargaze

of yearn

as

telepathic and kinetic energy(ies)

converge in hallow

a 7/6 chord

methodically melodious is the discord of the

stare in setting son   rest

assured

like myself

in a

crepuscular serenity

a realm of dropper manifest

&

devoid of meat puppet predeterminism

in the

chess of divine voyeurism

&

devoid of hierophant politics

&

the various ironies that perpetuate in a

seeming necessity

&

devoid of the heartbreaking and acknowledged constancy, the generally unchallenged continuity of systemic corruption and failure in politics & the judicial and criminal establishments

devoid of the illogical & self-denying beliefs as deprecatory & de-void of prejudice and those who lack gratitude for life as breathing real whether good or bad

6.

in a nocturne

      i lost myself

        anonymously pacified

          by a purchased

palliative gesture

&

like myself

confessional

face-plant

&

cigarette

analect(s)

percussion

two perfectly shaped ice cubes

& fragile in its evanescence

this peace

aperitif

harlot

synthesis placating

a carnal heart

charnel brushstrokes

club soda

into awake again

with myopic hope

resounding

a still

undisclosed

moral fiber

junk shot

drop cloth

too long in a day soon

in the someday

what's that sound

underscored atrocities

of a

harmonious carnality

cello wrought

heartstrings

a captive cake eaten

her diaphanous shroud

death and the maiden

the justines and magdelenas

in cliched literary vitiation

carnal heart & seething

sentient insurgence of ethereal seeping thru life and death

while assisted in breathless breathing

by baker's trumpet manifesting an

embraceable you

here on the ground

cellophane

anyone of you could have

been anyone   overpaint

in how many ways was the cross
         a didactic paradigm
                  with or without the crimes of christ
                           &
suffocating morals
         in an iniquitous eschatology
                  as such the criminal chimes of delusion
in

                           tainted meat
                  a bad cake, that
                  son of incubus

& sacrificial mary
         of a disembodied pardon

                           prerequisite
                  here on the ground without you
                           tyranny of time
                           seven horses
                           veritas
                           the enquirer
                           beat
                  guard yourself well from falling
                  as children in relation to the country

& to the violent oppression & guilty misgivings

in a genuine emptiness

had to cut the guilt

and embrace emptiness

and/or

intoxication

again

she had looked very beautiful

in an honest and vulnerable

moment as she said

you're never there

she was a liability

and just this passenger drives on and away

a logical cut and dried and a poetical insouciance

in the time of youth   smoke-rings and brandy
boots

a cigar lit   in the seat of thought   with a

holly tree above as savior from a rain that lights on

a travelled foliage   effulgence in an

influence of autumnal meanderings
forestral

chameleonic on the cobblestones of a thruout route

the harbors and musical festivities of mild new england

instrumentations   and pure sea foam

        and you look up and feel sky   and the crisp of
face plant

sidewalk naps in jersey   pennsylvania   virginia beach
      & east coast beaches & up winding lighthouses
         of meandering nature walks & city streets &
caverns
           the wildlife refuges   the taverns &
the boat tours
dig the architectured cafes   bookstores & eateries
    cathedrals   & such the feeling beauty of
       mountains
         islands
          waterfronts

(a) sweetness of hindsight lingers in some of a perfect
      dichotomy of experience in travel and all a beloved
       revery and to return

as societal standards of success run contrary to my happiness
personal nonchalance
    here on the ground without
      like myself & strangered
       soul-like
         & some weird sin

sifted sands
      canvassed and mosaical
          alone together
               sounded strike of ebony
                  &
                            it stoned me

thelonious as percussive
        by no means
             just staring interludes
                of pace yourself for me
                    & in attempt to feel
the emotions
      felt in waves
          intoxicated or other
          it is wordy paint
            such a bass line
              any avenue
                  chameleonic while un-
able to relate to
what an anywhere and roadless ephemeral

              something in the way
               is that feel
                &
            have you seen the sunset

as

each word in the prose

a poetic brush stroke

&

example of

posthumous remorse

PART TWO

you're never there

PART TWO PROLOGUE

many years ago, in my late teens i had written a novel, and somewhere in the semi-autobiographical narrative, i'd written about the ubiquity of suicidal passion in the anti-hero's subconscious throughout his exploits and excesses, & concerning these passions, i'd quoted hemingway, "there was much wine, an ignored tension, and a feeling of things coming that you could not prevent happening."

1

reason looks to her sweat on the forehead, needs cooled, as she says -he'd been here-and momentarily-. partial sunlight hits the table and lights on the sheetrock fallen of the fisted art on the wall, and she fingertips it to see if it's of any use.

the state of dopedick sees her for the ubiquitous liability awaiting her release from   but specific to a mildly sadistic sense of entertainment, he delays her departure from.

the apartment is oddly kept in an overt dichotomy of existences

sporadic placement of modestly artistic area rugs spread round about and folded in corners upright   on along beige walls with poetically aphoristic phrasings in black marker and broken mosaics where emotional paroxysms struck.

to the left of the antiquated sound system and up against the window are emptied canvasses of meticulous overpaint steadied up on an older keyboard stand and along the walls perimeter and on charcoal crates are classic books and art portfolios.

and in the corner opposite is found a makeshift chessboard with NABOKOV scrawled in black with transparent pieces.

the consistent what the fuck in her eyes   of clammy detachments   drift thru the room while taking notice of nothing   her eyes like a canvass   of without thought brushstrokes   and the urgencies of just in passing   she says -he's blasé blasé blasé too.-

        reason looks out the window and out thru the parking lot to the dumpster. days ago, while drinking scotch and soda to broken bicycles and others by waits, he'd economized his trips to recycling by leaving 12 bottles of beer next to the dumpster.

        a short, thin, dark-skinned cat had approached him and demanded

-are you a cop!?- -not at all-   -why you dressed correct, drinking with a dumpster?   -lost my family-   they shook hands and he moved on.

        the girl picks up a rosary that was inadvertently severed at the base and looks to reason with questions. he looks back -i am not an instrument of god.-   he knows she'll heavy overthink that.

        within the acoustics of the two rooms of the apartment and the darkened shadings on the wall of paradigm(s) in paint prose mosaics

        of what avails perpetual creation   or the continuity of man

i do not   the graphics of crosses translated   and gravities of a real gone   the damage done   always keep my head in my presence   and remorseless   a violence of primal instincts (an) flowers of evil   and   is it wrong to say you're wrong and am i wrong and who can dismiss the whole of the generations and in a day soon as island unto self and without aura and in the someday of that sound in silencing an always   a fuck not lest ye be fucked   and fuck well in fucking as nothing in nothing for nothing   and life viable and certainly   live in unadulterated certainty and affirmations logical in gratitude   and in dangers of mass meat puppetry misanthropic hurt in regards   man's inhumanity to man

and

HOLY BIBLE

COLISEUM

GESTAPO

GUILLOTINE

heart-

breaking rage as indiced by

camus   the stranger

mailer   the siege of chicago

hemingway   chapter 30 a farewell to arms

scrawled distinct and bold amidst the shadings of the walls.

reason looks to the mirror and into wolf-like piercing blue-green eyes

remembering what he'd said -nothin but love for you-   some days ago now, while peacefully purchasing bricks of junk and good hard cook from anonymous at his household where congregated matters of peace need be made. -the hoods got nothin but love for you   we see what you try to do-. and privacy had said pleasantly -red, blue, white   red, blue, white   its one love to you   i'm tryna keep you out the crossfire-.

dark-haired girl comes into the bathroom where reason stands before the mirror and sits to his right on the seat of the toilet. she shutters inwardly and looks up to him. he hands her two stamps. she begins to set and sighs long   -you contacted your attorney? reason stares a little colder and -he doesn't want the case. he's opposed to the abuse of drugs and the abuse of the invasion of privacy clause- her back stiffens and he looks to her -the police raids, they only found some stamps, i walked before court, municipal   you're good, babe-

reason black markers the wall above the toilet as dark-haired girl sucks his cock   anyone of you could have been anyone.

above the NABOKOV chessboard, he had markered a societal note concerning sex scandals in churches and modern surveillances, specifically since humans have evolved to the point that it's an acknowledged fact that a belief in a god is irrational, how is it in a technological globe with extensive surveillances, that any one priest could sexually assault any one minor, let alone the thousands of incidents per year? how is it not an investigated, cut and dried, and clear as day, guilty as fuck?

DOUBLY PROTECT THOSE KIDS

IMPRISON etc THOSE PRIESTS

rosemary's green eyes are a blue and grey as she ascends the top of the stair with a half-spent candle and looks to reason whose right hand is resting on the dark-haired girl's asshole.

she puts ice cream in the freezer and the candle on the cocktail table before leaving out.

the foundational ambiance of the apartment can be applied many adjectives, inasmuch as they contradict the ambience of their meaning as they subtract from the soul, logic, and self of it. you breathe in the lack of harrow and the suffocating adjectives of non-descript. it takes the appalling fuck of too much to breathe it in.

as bro appears up the steps with eyes quickly evasive to any direction he looks in and sets on the grey of the couch, and before he nods, he says and smirking -had consistently bid eight   when you can't not got wheels   there's no music to it-.

bro and reason get high and as bro nods, reason recalls in a resignation to the pain of it, the death of his nodding friend's wife, as in the confusion of his addiction he'd handed to his wife the hot dose of junk that reason, in an acquiescing suicide, had requested. there are absolutely no words to describe the feeling reason has in being there for his friend. it just is and he is there, without ever trying to suit the non-descript of it.

rosemary, undeniably beautiful and vulnerable asks   -will you marry me?

an indescribable emptiness exhausts reason to the thoughtful desire for a more specific evasiveness that he could eventually be held accountable for. in the search for words and feeling and without tact, the moments pass and nothing more is said.

days of detox and writings.

remedies, recipes, club soda

the man remembers everything, or rather everything it is he doesn't remember.

he does remember nothing.

the exact totality of all.

again.

or it else be that in glimpses.

methamphetamine good cook

and bro showed up with better

baking soda and laxatives

straws and sour candy

cough syrup aperitifs

chocolates and menthol

fresh syringes and alcohol swabs

after the drop.

bro explains to reason that reason had slapped rosemary across the room and kicked her down the stairs   the lucidity of a fix and within his nod of clarifying reflection(s)

as in at the piano a melodious redundancy of never changing and prompts of a perpetual and remorseless act unending

she had cried brokenly for our baby unborn before falling silent

as on the path taken by the moccasins the man had stood in when he had forgotten momentarily as to why he did not commit suicide

she lay no longer looking up and bro had made some calls on the immediate to guarantee reason's safety once imprisoned

he never explained why the cops had made no arrest after she'd been stabilized and hospitalized

with understood aryan and mafia connections unstated

and there it is.

the

our baby.

the sound of a heart breaking.

that blunt dull and resonating pain that sounds in search for irrevocable exhale

exacting precious tears fallen on an open wound

and in thru acts of autonomy where thoughts can never again

approach

just another spectre of a shadow taking each methodical step with you as each moment cared for meticulously while the anatomy atrophies in a frame by frame unfolding of career addict degeneration and paroxysmal spasms and sharp in the central nervous system.

as what lingers in the constancies of recent memory, reason's pre-apartment household downtown where the dichotomous aspects of his existence found no singular peace and in thru the inevitable crescendo where rosemary had left with their daughter in escape from his violent drinking, and reason had stared into an old, small, circular mirror that had previously had tabs of acid secured to its back hidden from sight and he had frequented rails of cocaine and heroin on its face, reason fully internalized the peace of a principled and genuine, lifelong emptiness.

and as within his composition(s) of self, he finished his daily jug of scotch, injected the junk, realized he was out of beer, stood up to go to the store, and fell out.

and in the poetic jugular of the apartment's situated circumferences of a singular vigil of his life's dichotomies, he stares out the window across the parking lot of his resolute lack of avenue and inhales the four sticks of wet, smoking in resolutely calm succession of a formaldehyde embalming and induced kaleidoscopic hallucinatory trance, and recedes as slipping peacefully into an abject permanency.

a nietzschean afterworld as the breathing recurrences before the autonomies of consciousness are finally exhausted.

PART THREE

formatted absence

PART THREE
PROLOGUE

granted, unless jesus was absolutely insane, he would have known
that heaven and hell are parabolic concepts & in thru his crim-
inally fanatic teachings and probable performance art(s) passed
down via documented creativity and translations, he's conned billions of people into commemorating him via symbolic cannibalism with his proverbial balls on their chin.

nietzsche was worried, understandably so, that there would be a
potentially chaotic nihilism when people fully realized that there
is no logic in the belief in god. i believe he would be happy to note,
as i am happy to note, that in 8 of the 10 safest countries in the

world, the majority of the population is atheist or non-religious. and while there are some factors in countries that would have to be considered and some varying specifics in the percentages themselves, all of the countries have in the very least, had a significant decrease in those who believe in god.

it stands to reason, naturally, that where there is logic and certainty, there's potential for peace, and more appreciation for life as is, and you are free of the subconscious guilt that your morals and prejudices etcetera are fundamentally baseless.

there's the potential for humanity and expression, they can foster what's good and adapt in survivalism and productivity, people can genuinely look at themselves and strive as individuals of varying potential.

naturally, people need to be moral as individuals in collectively ethical communities. what individual of honestly good heart and morality believes in hell?

i cannot be a part of a philosophy that believes in hell, as undeniably creative and childish in their fiction, it breaks my heart that a people contrived something that's endlessly cruel in its inhumanity to man.

as to consider the secondary points considering the lack of logic and the complete lack of evidence concerning gods existence.

there is the absurdity of ephysian predestination and the intrusions of a divine voyeurism.

theists rarely acknowledge what was written in bible and scripture and largely attempt to justify it by stating their own translation of the words so as to palliate their judgment for if the bible is to considered a literal testament and decree, how many theists would see eternal reward?

how is it not just another example of how asinine it is to place any credence into scripture if and since so many in organized religion daily soften or otherwise alter the very words written?

how are we not a sadistic creators meat puppets and pawns?

and how is the concept of satan not the concept of gods scapegoat?

just as its not logically possible that a moses parted a sea, it's not possible that scriptures god exists and created the world. there is no specific evidence that moses existed.

granted, if a god is omnipotent and omniscient, he is all-powerful and all-knowing, and no paradox etcetera would then be beyond his solving. and those who put forth cute dissertations explaining how god cannot be both omniscient and omnipotent should rather than further their onanistic findings just approach the topic at its baseless foundation and point out that both omnipotence and omniscience are nothing more than concepts.

and granted, omnipotence and omniscience are just as unscientific and fictional a concept as god is. no one can prepare an understanding based on anything factual, in regards the existence of those three concepts. it's all childish prattle. how, logically, is it not all just garrulous onanism? it's largely for those who congregate to discuss philosophical concepts and establish themselves as a jones without having said very much of anything at all and granted, were the scriptures god to exist, the creator of the world, he created all, knows all, and can do or has done all. just as he created all and everything good, he created all and everything evil. the all-encompassing all, as in every facet and factor of every single aspect of every single individual in and of itself, and as a collective totality, whether conceptual or otherwise, or foundational realities or factors therein.

all.

how then is he not responsible for satan, as concept or belief. how is satan not gods scapegoat? that he then administers his will as to his instruments as pawns or individual meat puppets in his divine comedic and tragic chessboard of his fiat in all in every way, with a conceptual evil as scapegoated satan, for the constituents of his will, as meat puppet individuals obliging to his doing as he sees fit, and blame the concept of satan for his in all ways fiat and will.

beyond illogical theistic conveniences and specifically stated, were god to exist, then it does no good to attempt to say that he cannot absolve evil and suffering, or that he is unaware of evil and suffering, and moreover, that he did not create evil and suffering.

and granted, the attempt to blame the free will of the people is as scapegoat and unscientific. as, in and of itself, free will is factually, an illusion and is biblically negated by scripture in ephysians, another creative concept and cute as psychological phenomenon in addition to the definitions of omnipotence and omniscience as they are applied to a god as creator of the world.

this all stated, were god to exist, he is sadistic and we, his meat puppets.

moreover, there is no scientific evidence in support of the concepts of god, heaven, hell, omnipotence, omniscience, etc. and in regards, free will, no one is as yet saying much of anything definitive, as a predicate to what end exactly? as in a moral assessment, individuals should damn well realize that they can and should decidedly utilize their will and cultivate their energies. as the sciences regarding free will could only ultimately prove more congruent, naturally, to atheism.

how can you expect a nation to be largely logical and stable in politics and legislature etcetera if the large majority of citizens are christians or others that hold the belief that unless you symbolically cannibalize jesus, you will suffer the endless cruelties of the concept of hell? and how, logically, was jesus, as son of god and a virgin, not a suicide? it's completely disgusting that there might possibly be one individual on the globe capable of giving credence to any aspect of the overt contradictory impossibilities in a completely judgmental and wildly cruel work of fiction that has historically influenced an intense amount of global insanity and has been the incendiary crux of the extreme depravity in the ongoing religious wars. i want no part of it, and am un-nerved to note that according to modern research, some 75% of my fellow countrymen believe there is heaven and hell. it may be cozier for some modern-day individuals who do desire a safer and logical existence to temporarily attend church rather than face the rather undeniable fact that such a countless body count has been attributed to wars over religion and have factually been lost for absolutely no reason other than the inherent and primal need for sex and violence.

with no evidence of its existence, how can one good and sane individual believe in the endless cruelties of hell?

how can there be global peace expected when 1/3 of the population baselessly believes that the other 2/3 will burn endlessly after death?

how am i, for example, to feel safe being governed, judged, taught etcetera by a someone that believes that i am going to hell?

how is an atheist to feel unjudged and safe amidst a christian whose profession is one of power?

how is that not dangerous?

how were they seen fit for the profession? and by whom? of what belief? and basis to it?

granted, i'm not concerned with hell, as there is no evidence of its existence, i am concerned with the irrational instability of the individuals that believe in that conceptual inhumanity, and as to how they obtained a position of power.

if your values and morals, let alone prejudices and judgements are rooted since childhood in a christian or other belief in hellfire and the other baseless and irrational beliefs involving a god or gods, then certainly you are prone and likely to be illogical in other aspects of life.

the wildly creative fiction that is bible including the wildly influential and unrepentant philosopher, jesus of nazareth has been repeatedly hit, its roast beef.

global example of such numerous accounts of cities and towns in numerous states and countries, and in each town, numerous community churches conveniently splicing or omitting variations of translated historical fiction to suit the differing temperaments of individual belief.

its fundamentally unstable to bring children up on violent fiction.

there has never been a more impactful and boldly influential philosopher as jesus of nazareth.

logically, it would be tragic if he were as unstable as aspects of his fiction are baseless. such as his childish insistence in condemning all those who would not agree with him, and were it a twisted and insightful sick sense of humor that jesus had, then i only give props, and say, cheers, you motherfucker.

as parents, and granted that the children are the future, how is it genuinely good and stable to base your parental opinions, morals, prejudices etcetera on an extremely violent fiction with baseless concepts?

i do not trust the heart or the intentions let alone the humanity or the moral and logical stability of anyone or any community or establishment that believes in hell, or that believes in heaven and hell.

what religious individual with any self-respect could attempt to negate the undeniably irrefutable absence of humanity and the baselessness of their belief in the conceptual fictions?

to be further strictly heartfelt in logic and to be concise and without much repetition, in having focused primarily on the cut and dried certainty of biblical immoralities and the baselessness at its foundation, i don't see how any genuinely good-hearted and sane individual could give the bible and other organized religions much thought, let alone, credence.

logically, how is it stable and good-hearted, to put the innocence of a child before a statue etcetera of a largely naked, brutally beaten and executed outlaw philosopher? and inform the child that they must symbolically cannibalize this man to save their soul in absolution of things that they by no means have done, else they suffer unending fires etcetera in hell?

were any one of the remarkably terrifying billions of christians able to provide scientific evidence to support their belief in god, it could only prove tremendously worse for the inhabitants of the world. there would then be billions of justified cruel and prejudiced individuals rapping on in variants of convenient translations of scripture about parabolic morality and literal codes of conduct, that if not accepted and adhered to, you must cleanse the soul in absolution of guilt by symbolic cannibalism. naturally there are many of those billions that don't apply any belief to the literal nature of hell and god and just go about the work of life and wasting their time as opposed to finding themselves and what it is they are about as individuals before a sunday gathering etcetera.

i'm not about drinking jesus, by any means. i would not cannibalize jesus, let alone, accept certain aspects of his teaching.

logically and fortunately, for those of genuinely good heart and humane decencies, it remains irrational to believe in baseless conceptual fictions.

and congruent to humanity, there is not one individual in history that deserves to burn endlessly.

and if this god of omniscience and omnipotence exists, trust and believe he doesn't give a fuck about what one of his created meat puppets has to say or do in acceptance or rejection of his will, as he alone would have willed it or foreseen the opposing sciences and philosophies, all the prattling earthly intellectual digestions that meat puppet individuals express in any attempt to negate or support any of his concepts that he instilled or allowed to be instilled would be completely foreseen implementations of his doing as he sees fit to do, just as this god as creator is in all ways the way, the very essence in all essential or otherwise components of every and anything. this god doesn't give a fuck that theists consistently fail to genuinely understand the very definitions of the terminologies they use to apply their faith, and this god would have created their inability to see the logical aspects of how the definitions of the words they use to apply their faith logically negate the faith itself as in another example of mediocrity and it's cannibalistic rhetoric. theres only so many ways to paint a pig. and life and nature is such an extraordinarily beautiful thing

 only religious individuals could delude themselves in ask for afterlife in a dissatisfaction and negation of existing and appreciating life as is, for good or ill.

how has the irrational foundation not been of negative impact? and in how many ways has it been?

who, with logical self-respect is satisfied with the judicial system?

who would attempt to deny that every day, there are numerous factors culminating in unjustifiable results in a remarkably large number of cases?

and who could expect otherwise from a people whose foundation is baseless?

it stands to reason that a people of fundamental baselessness would grow more and more casual in their acceptance of other aspects of the irrational.

how can anyone expect logical legislation from a politic of baseless foundation?

why is abject idiocy overtly accepted and applauded in the entertainment media?

why, logically, is there a war on drugs? as it is one that repeats the same mistakes over and over again expecting different results.

why are the jails and prisons consistently populated with non-violent offenders?

why, logically, do we not work to implement the gradual legalization of most illicit drugs?

and put the money made by natural and uncut corporations with paid labor workers towards prevention, awareness, and outreach, in the name of gradual peace and safety for the individuals of society and its law enforcement, and eliminating facets of gang wars and drug wars etcetera?

did we learn nothing from prohibition?

yeah, why?

why not a logical war against violence?

why not districts of peaceful and optional segregations as an addition to promoting equal rights and an end to hate crimes and racisms?

why the absolute fuck is prostitution illegal?

how does that protect the sex workers and how could it genuinely attempt to negate supply and demand?

and moreover, why?

protect and legalize the sex workers, and respectfully have them internalize the respect they deserve.

apply heart in logic in all ways and etcetera.

PART FOUR

a

volume

of

painted prosody

(a note on the painted prosody)

in applying and securing a peace in my dichotomous exist-
ence(s)

    & very specific to a posthumous internalization
that it's borrowed time & a peaceful remorse without binding
senses of guilt or conscience

after

having

decades lived

disorganizing and altering the senses in life-perception

(see rimbaud, baudelaire, blake, kesey, huxley, jim morrison
etc)

                to then

an enforced cold turkey detox and years in jail
                                                after having

the growing appreciation(s) for life as is

& exhausted after
                the multiple flat-lining overdoses
                        i felt to isolate the energies of life as
                        a tribute to it
life-affirming isolations of appreciation and experience

                                        & undertones of in-
strumentation

orchestral foliage & shining
                calms the clowns of chthonic   passage
                        and robert johnson   in a
cobblestone theatre   and   clean sets
                a light such beautiful   touching thru   and heard
                        in the seeking steps   and the

kinetic energy   in that feel of

        conveyed insights   and d.a. levy

              & what you need?   as

symposium(s) of karma   the block

        universe(ally)

            the syndicates who got

              proprietary and all the immoralities

                  of the sensate

                    and

                  the sentient

                  invariably altered

      it was early in the affair & such a memorable expres-
sion she had, that i could only describe as that of so many ques-
tions she would never ask   as she stood there   & looking at me

      while i stood in the shower with the tie undone in a
full suit with a cup of coffee and a cigarette & assuring her that
everything is ok & as the water from the shower head hit me in
the chest and the residual effects of my alcohol and cocaine fueled
weekend with a friend and some girls we'd met at a bar on

the east coast was starting to materialize into the charming com-
placencies of cliched axioms of denial

in thru the exacting sentience of life-sensation

      to exact (an) singularity of self

        (as) oneness   and peace principled

do you know the feeling
energy(ies) of the non-descript?
a life-sensation & pin-pointed
do you know the feeling
energy(ies) of paroxysm?

in between or bridge is a soma
and the fundamental differences between beatifying
a healthy fusion of dionysian and apollonian energies
and/or
epicurean and relatively moderate hedonism
&
as bridge or between is a soma
and
do you know the feeling & energy
of deja-vu?
and to assimilate in appreciation
of its factors   all aspects
encapsulating evanescence

& securing in gratitude
the beatified
the hierophanies of singularity

the peace(able) ability
           to isolate   the sound
                     to feel   in hearing
      a singing wind   in thru which   the
procession down
           (an) individual and spiraling
                      autumn leaf   takes to the ground
      and the touch is heard

as

         aspects of nature   and that clarity
              the feeling energy(ies)
of (an) intrinsic reality

   after years of dating her as her live in man   and the specific
omission(s) of emotion   i introduced her to a friend of mine
and she looked at him & saying   it's nice to meet you

   i then said to her   you might as well say the same thing to me
we were all sitting in the living room and it was the first time i had
spiked junk in front of her   my friend laughed a little   again

   i, by no means, can describe an understanding of the curious
and wondering & the essentially shocked   emotional honesty
she beautifully expressed   and without words

                              sensate discovery(s)

with some distance from thought
primeval
&
clearly atavistic
the
inchoate prerequisites of within

the correlating relevance
a revelry of sound   as a muted feeling energy
(an) applied divinity
the image(s) & the emotive horn

as subsistence in a form of such canvassing elements
of an intrinsic transference of focus
applying specific(s) of sensory logic
and clairvoyant
delineating the specified energy(ies)
of life-sensation

in the focus of the emotional melody
of contemplative memory
do you know   or can you relate   in appreciation(s)
exacting the moment
of your heart breaking
the seething and the binding
of emotional exertion

the heartful exigence
the very essence
of the isolated
&
so exigent
ache(ing)
life-sensation

encapsulate

the raptured sonorities of the sensate

that which led to the

etymologies & sciences
of isolating thought in freedom(s)
of orgasmic moment(s)

the energy(s) of orgasm

& the sensory perception(s)

of the addict's moments right before

the release(s) of an applied fix

& denizens of explosive violence

& their isolated energy(ies)

on their momentous journey toward paroxysm

& the peace(able) clarity within a dichotomy

i feel the time comes or it doesn't

provided a person is open to it

the weathered and peaceful compromise

or moderation

of having clarified and accepted the self as to

good and evil

yin and yang

apollonian and dionysian

& the so duplicitous majesties of nature

so as to attempt and feel an understanding

of aspects of the immensities in the

synergy of nature

such an appalling and painfully egregious insult   that man observes what aspects he has   of the immensities of nature   and its enduring & encapsulating synergy   and man attempts to give irrational credence to the fictional concepts of gods and god in an undeniably illogical ingratitude

and insult to nature

nature IS

&

undeniable

as imperturbably resolute in essentially

all of the attributes that man has offered in his fiction

nature never has and will never need man
      & when man in its human nature gets too cute
         and complicated with and for itself
     (as it has and again will)
            nature reacts & vehemently
  before the natural synergy
       that man is completely and irrevocably incapable of
         is naturally restored

there never has been & there presently isn't
     a peaceful synergy in man's politics & religions
       as man has never
          in his childish delusions and
pathetic ego
            acknowledged
nature

&

the sensory lack of emotions and feelings
                    after orgasmic release & not desirous of any
touch or word
                              the very energy(ies) of non-
descript & empty

ARTIST(s)
     in having
some understanding of these isolated
        extremes of energy
                in perceived & experienced emotive moments
an individual can begin to appreciate
        a balance in the very necessarily dichotomous
            self & real

            as an incorporated interpretation of correlated energies in
an   intersubjectivity (an) paradigm of yearning
        do you know the moment(s) of yearn & of perfunctory
circumference?
     the pinned measure(s) of hope   the very feeling of things left
unsaid?

as in a very sentient & ubiquitous feeling   of a breathing
posterity
            & i didn't know that the tears were falling

from my eyes as i overtly painted
what was and is and had been
i just consciously exhaled the exhaustion(s)

wurlitzers & pump organs & accordians
stray(ed) dances and abstracted
abstractions & soul-like
effigies of the real
while explosively innovative
& a sustain pedal to boot the extended in creativity
the hieronymus bosch overpaint

they danced as cyclical exigent(s) of intoxication
as sublimated correlations were expressed & vividly
the fluidity of motion conveyed the self-evi-
dent expletives
of feeling
their motions served the euphoria(s) of self
as self-contained & in hope for the continuities
of a dancing deliquescence
as in the singular moment(s) of time passing
eudaemonic in a crepuscular experience

the dug and assimilated
the ascertained and enveloped
the dances of speech felt & paintings heard

expressing the feel in sentient moment(s)
     of a lorca or a cummings painted by a renoir
        a dali   a basquiat a degas a de kooning
          the canvassing choreographies
area rugs to sound the track
     in a very conscious spontaneity
        the brush begins on lighting as
          the opening percussive sounds
& coltrane starts in as
     the encapsulating somehow(s)
        of preludes and overtures
          of wine and chopin and schubert

in violinic stare
     as in goethe & that feel of cello wrought
        & heartstrings melancholic
          & various epiphanous dances
as sustaining eyes open
     in their art & their self-evident moment(s)
     of nature's very now

& credits roll on composition(s) of now
     & déjà vu in clarity(ies) of karmic revery
     & as now & the left behind

as a passenger in palliatives

      and thru the exigence of creation

            & synchronicities of self and shadow
with all the occupational hazards sublimated in the tranquil-
ity(ies)

         of differing cobblestones & refuges of nature

     of glass bottom boat tours & sifting waters & sands on
beaches

       of the peaceful & the immense energy(ies) of et-
cetera

sock theory

                               LOOK

have you noticed in how many respects   that so many people
make the exact same gestures and say the exact same things?
given a certain prompt or situation   what is it in them?   the
sciences of the herd mentality? certain inherent deficiencies and
mediocrities? has it to do with a psychological phenomenon involving reactionary impulses in brain chemistries? do you realize
that it's not very difficult to isolate what prompts prompted what
percentage of a certain population to react this identical way or
that?   and to then create the situations in which those certain
prompts had identical reactions, to pave the way and create the
results? it isn't very difficult to then prepare an understanding
of the predictabilities of mediocrity and manipulate the results
whether calculating responsive algorithms, or intuiting and gain-
ing perspective as to the responsive when and specifically why.

                               &

MIND YOU

poems of a (magik) created
    soliloquies of feeling
        with words as brush-strokes
to paint the brush-strokes of soliloquy

& in magical application of phrases
    & correlation(s) felt in the applied sounds
        as soundtracking
            specifying aspects of musicianship as in
the melodic discord of a staccato 7/6 chord
    as the paint brush stabs the canvass
        with the adjectives that colour
the soliloquy(ies) in the conveyed artisan(s) incantation

                &

the subconscious stream of observing & what is sensed & in palpable gestures   there's a constant and disconcerting inability to relate & both embarrassed for the performer and for those enjoying the performance

and emptied further by the so few variations in sect by sect within the parameters of the emotion that the performances intend to evoke   each sect the same very many and same very few variations of responsive expressions and gesticulations with very same body language

and while the good performers would be aware enough certainly to intuit what need conveyed to prompt the desired responses   what aspect of the performer and its audience involves self-respect?

what i see and it un-nerves me   is that your performance art is simply the concrete & crafted power(s) of manipulation

your tragedians and comedians alike   & while it certainly isn't entertaining to me to observe a comedian prattle in repe- tition   the contextual prompts they've crafted utilizing their assimilated intuitions and foresights into a methodically scripted performance art   they should damn well think in terms of self- respect & apply their power over their audiences of predictably prompted response and gesture   in ways congruent to affirm- ations of life & evolving morality(s) & a conveyed methodical script that either enhances or awakens

&

what aspect of self-respect or life-affirming purpose is in the critic as sycophant in view of blood money   what is it in their overt self- importance that feels it necessary to judge others?

&

what is it or what lack is it in the fan that could conceivably find another individual to be something to etcetera about? trust and believe that the performer knows exactly what its doing & in the realm(s) of echelon in which the artisans of manipulating expres- sion(s) of theatre and cinema & musical and performance art   the art(s) of manipulating its audiences applied just as undeniably as those of mediocrity are inherently incapable of discerning their inability(s) of awareness   they cannot isolate their emotions in order to understand them   they cannot think outside the given formatting with any determined intent to isolate & prepare an understanding of the conceptual or emotional political angles they lack the ability to sense the energies intent in order to con- sciously intuit whether to succumb to emotionally or to distrust and deflect the artistic inclination   all in the audience are affected & the affecting influence can & very often does have genu- inely pervasive results   impacting residential and governmental politics

&

within the echelon(s) the crafted artist can only manipulate as
long as its own primal stability and health allows & is constantly
aware of the parameters of circumstance & its audiences inherent propensity to find their artist just as spent & washed up as
they had found them innovative & ingenious these propensities
while largely unprompted are foreseen and are as predictable as
the prompted responses & generally its simply another artist con-
trolling the audiences rapt attention & emotional nod

look at the canvass

    see thru it to the images of its

        reflected & visceral countenance

the textured & mosaical 1/16th of isolated vision

    the parameters of embroidered thought

        in kaleidoscopic frames

of sidereal intoxications as architecture & feeling

    in declarative mandala(s)

        of a specifying abstract & supernal vitality

& illustrious

    the searching eyes

        & rapt in liquescent reservoirs

          of borgesian luminosity

give color to bass drum denotation
        & architectured shadings
            & hues to rhapsodic circumference
apply to the canvass the sidereal motion(s)
        as though what felt in a
            measured musical adage
a comforting loop of (an) experienced progression
        &

while the minor of controlled feedback from the
        distorted electric guitar is rhythmically pulsing
        with underscored appreciation(s)

&

     as

the stand-up bass maintains its course of acoustic measure
        the baby grand offers notes specifically melodic
            in accompaniment & specific counter to
it's sporadic and meditative discords as
        correlating resonant to the guitar's controlled corusca-
tion(s)
            of driving measure & cool in d minor
a dubbed & percussive analect of ancient origin
        the sudden acoustics of nylon strings of arpeggio pick
            & the sonorous serenity(ies) of c minor

& the seraphity(ies) of f minor

& the piano's divination(s) of a minor

of a somehow numb

& with sporadic raps of steel & slide

& all in the arrangement meander thru

the subtleties of (a) navigated intricacy

the paced variations as congruent to the crux

& converge at the ethereal crossroads

where the emotive sounding(s) of the

strings of cello make their offerings

as the brush puts to canvass

the very color of heartache

&

so

do you know

the evanescent euphoria(s)

in smoke of the iced hot pull

of

cocaine

in

good cook?

the meticulated excesses of thematic nocturne

the posthumous remorse

in the autonomous resurrection

is artistic player piano

&

this passenger is taking

his satisfying calm

of another non-descript out

towards the western crepuscular serenity(ies)

&

how beautiful

&

how sickly fuckin beautiful it is

for those of us in whom have it

hope